Shadows on the Barn

Sarah Garland

Berrrk?!*

Young Lions

First published in Great Britain by
A & C Black (Publishers) Ltd 1990
First published in Young Lions 1991

Young Lions is an imprint of the Children's Division,
part of HarperCollins Publishers Ltd,
77–85 Fulham Palace Road, London W6 8JB

Copyright © Sarah Garland 1990

Printed and bound in Great Britain by
HarperCollins Book Manufacturing, Glasgow

Conditions of Sale
This book is sold subject to the condition
that it shall not, by way of trade or otherwise,
be lent, re-sold, hired out or otherwise
circulated without the publisher's prior
consent in any form of binding or cover other
than that in which it is published and without
a similar condition including this condition
being imposed on the subsequent purchaser.

CHAPTER 1

Strangers

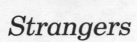

Those two men gave me a fright. They were big and heavy, but they'd come through the bushes without a sound.

'A dozen eggs?' I said.

'That would do nicely mate,' said
one, looking all around, sucking a
cigar and taking out a fat wallet.

'Keep the change mate,' he said.

My customers never say 'keep the change'. They count their pennies in this village.

5

'I didn't like them Mum,' I said that
night at supper.

Mum was distracted, making a
sculpture out of orange-peel and a
fork. She never stops, not even at
mealtimes.

'Ned my darling,' she murmured,
'I'm sure that's the last we'll see
of them.'

How wrong she was!

CHAPTER 2

The Menace Begins

Next morning I went to school with my friend, Izzy.

'Those men were crooked and crafty,' I said.

'Sneaky and snakey,' said Izzy.

'Will you help me deliver eggs after school?' I asked.

'O.K.' she said.

Izzy often comes home with me.
Her parents work late.

Delivering eggs takes a long time because everybody gives us something to eat.

Half a dozen, Mrs Brassica.

Thank you my dears. Do take a bun.

By the time we were on our way
home it was late and we were full to
bursting. Then we saw it.
That smooth black car.

It came cruising past us down the lane from our house, as silent as a hunting cat. The windows were dark so we couldn't see inside, but

the smell of cigar smoke drifted back between the hedges

CHAPTER 3

Sign or Else

We raced home to find Mum
chipping hard at a statue. Her face
was red, and chips of stone were
flying like firework sparks.

You were right about those men! Just look at this!

'They said the roof was rotten and it was against the law to let old buildings fall down,' cried Mum. 'They want to turn the barn into luxury flats. When I said no, they got very nasty!'

CONTRACT

I, Sally Carter, hereby declare that Jake Dodge and Samuel Racket shall be owners of Hen Barn forever

Signed . . . . SIGN HERE

I love that old barn. I play there a lot. My chickens scratch up all kinds of treasures there. Most of the things in my treasure box come from the barn.

'Have *we* got enough money to
mend the barn roof ?' I asked.

'No, we have not,' said Mum.

I remembered that I hadn't had any
pocket money for about two years.
I supposed Mum was right.

From that day on, things began to
go wrong.

Mice in my gumboots.

Flat tyres on my bike.

My cub uniform gone.

The drain blocked and the kitchen flooded.

CHAPTER 4

Kidnapped

Next day I was passing Mum's
sculpture when I saw . . .

Mum was in despair.

And every day those crooks sent us
another nasty letter.

Now comes the worst part.

I opened the hen house one morning
as usual to find . . .

. . . half my chickens had vanished!
It was the last straw.

'Calm down,' said Izzy.
'We need a plan.'

All day long I was distracted.
My teachers got fed up with me.

At the end of the day, Mrs Logg said,

CHAPTER 5

Hatching a Plan

On the way home Izzy and I
thought up three plans.

We could dig a booby trap.

We could invent an electric
burglar alarm.

We could borrow a wolf from the zoo.

None of the plans were very good.

'We must protect the rest of the chickens,' I said.

'Let's sleep in the hen house then,' said Izzy.

We agreed to meet at eleven o'clock. I wished we had some weapons.

I put my alarm clock under my
pillow and tried to go to sleep.

Tick Tock

I heard Mum playing music
downstairs and

stoking the stove . . .

climbing the stairs . . .

running a bath . . . then . . .

I crept down the stairs. The kitchen
was warm, and dark as the coal hole.
I felt for the door latch.

The dew was like ice under my bare
feet. The moon sailed out from
behind the clouds and lit the yard.

The trees, the barn, Mum's statue,
they were different, they seemed to
breathe, to move. My skin prickled
all over.

CHAPTER 6

Danger

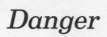

'Ned,' said a quiet voice right beside me.

'Oh Izzy! It's you!'

We climbed into the hen house.
The hens made comfortable
clucking noises and shuffled on
their perches.

Outside there were rustlings and
squeakings. The barn door creaked.
An owl hooted.

A car purred.

Already I could smell the horrible
scent of a cigar.

Outside, two enormous shadows moved against the moonlit wall of the barn. Closer they came, closer . .

. . . the hen house rocked as those big men leaned against it.

Got the rags, Sammy? And the paraffin?

And the matches, Jake.

The crooks had gone, but above the noise of their car we could hear a horrible crackling sound.

CHAPTER 7

Fire!

We hurled ourselves out of the hen house. There was no time to get Mum, no time for the fire brigade.

'The tap,' panted Izzy.
I grabbed the hose.
We fought the flames.

The grass hissed and smoked, the ground turned black, but at last the fire was out.

The hen house was saved!

Izzy and I staggered off to bed.
We'd stopped the crooks that night,
but what about tomorrow?

I had barely closed my eyes when
Mum shook me awake.

That was the best suggestion
Mum ever made.

CHAPTER 8

Ned's Treasure

'Ned Carter! Izzy Smith! Wake up at the back there!' cried Mrs Logg, rapping the table with someone's collection of ginger-beer bottles.

'Oh really Izzy! That's not good enough. What about you, Ned?'

'My treasure box, Mrs Logg,' I said.

Hmmm. Very nice, Ned.

Then Mrs Logg pounced!

Her hands were full of the little clay squares which my chickens scratch up from the barn floor.

Aha! What are these?

'Tessera! Tesserae!' breathed Mrs Logg.
'Stay there class! Don't move!
I'm going to ring the museum!'

She dashed out to the staffroom!

CHAPTER 9

The Hunt Is On

'Show us *exactly* where you found them, Ned,' said Mrs Logg. We were marching down our lane, me and Izzy at the front with Mrs Logg.

A little red car was waiting at our gate. A tall thin man got out and Mrs Logg sprang towards him.

'Dr Hanky! How good of you to come! Class, this is Dr Hanky, an eminent archaeologist from the museum.'

We all fell quiet in the barn. It was
odd to see so many people in my
private place.

I knelt down on that old floor and
began to scoop up the dusty earth.
Beezer watched me sideways.
She pecked up a wood louse.
The class leaned forward.

There was a sigh as I lifted up the
stones. One was bright blue, the
other a dusky red.

Dr Hanky fell on his knees beside
me and began to poke about
with a trowel.

At last he sat back and cleared
his throat.

This is
e REAL THING!

berrrk!

CHAPTER 10

Another Rescue

'What exactly do you mean,
Dr Hanky?' asked my mother.

'I mean,' said the tall, thin man, 'that there is a large Roman mosaic beneath your barn floor Mrs Carter. I would like your permission to excavate. We would pay you well of course.'

Dr Hanky sipped his coffee. 'We would also have to rebuild the barn roof to protect the mosaic. I hope you would not object to that?'

Mum smiled. 'Have another biscuit,' she said.

Izzy and I left them to it and set off back to school for lunch. Was it my imagination? Was there a faint whiff of cigar smoke in the air?

'Those crooks will never come back now,' cried Izzy. 'You are pleased aren't you Ned?'

'Of course I'm pleased,' I said,
'but I miss my chickens.'

59

We didn't have many eggs to sell after school.

Only six eggs, Mr Bold.

Half my chickens have been stolen.

Mr Bold looked slowly round.
'Funny,' he said. 'Come and see
what I've just found in my toolshed.
Someone must have dumped them
in there days ago.'

CHAPTER 11

Chickens Triumphant!

The archaeologists spent all summer holiday in our barn, uncovering the mosaic. Izzy and I made friends with them.

Mum has become great friends with
Dr Hanky. He's given her some
special glue for mending stone.

Izzy and I have got a new job now.

At weekends we get paid for showing our mosaic to the public. They often buy eggs, too, and sometimes statues.